I0533408

I Am the Story
I Was Afraid to Tell

A Poetic Memoir of Survival, Grief, and Becoming Me

Liliana
Caliente-Cazadora

I Am the Story I Was Afraid to Tell
A Poetic Memoir of Survival, Grief, and Becoming Me

Contact Information:

Liliana Caliente-Cazadora

@CazadoraLiliana

Official Website

author-liliana.com

This is a work of fiction. Names, characters, businesses, places, events, locales, and incidents are either the products of the author's imagination or used in a fictitious manner. Any resemblance to actual persons, living or dead, or actual events is purely coincidental.

Dedication

For the ones who made room for me
when I didn't know how to take up space.

For **Miguel**,
my little brother,
my reason to stay soft in a world that demanded I be hard.
Protecting you helped save me—
and watching you become the father we never had
is one of the greatest gifts of my life.

For **Uncle Sergio**,
who didn't ask for explanations—
just opened his door, made pancakes,
and taught me what safety could feel like.
Your silence was healing,
your presence, a shelter.

For **Diego**,
who will never know the kind of fear we grew up with—
you are the beginning of a new story,
the proof that cycles can be broken
and that love, when done right,
can grow up fearless.

And for every soul
who has carried their story in silence—
this book is for you.

You are not alone.
You are not to blame.
You are not what they did to you.

You are still here.
And that is everything.

Table of Contents

Dear Reader,

Thank you for being here.

Writing this book was one of the most difficult and healing things I've ever done. These poems come from some of the most painful and personal parts of my life , the parts I never thought I'd share with anyone, let alone put into a book.

For a long time, I didn't think my story mattered. I was afraid that speaking it out loud would make people look at me differently. I thought survival meant staying quiet. I thought strength meant not feeling anything.

But I was wrong. Telling the truth, even when your voice shakes, is one of the strongest things you can do. And feeling deeply doesn't make you weak. It makes you human.

If you're reading this and carrying something heavy, something unspoken, please know you are not alone. There is no shame in what you've survived. There is no expiration date on healing. And there is still beauty waiting for you, even if you can't see it yet.

This book is for anyone who has ever been afraid to tell their story. I hope it gives you comfort, courage, or even just a moment where you feel seen. You deserve to take up space. You deserve to be heard. And you deserve to love yourself as you are — not just after the healing, but even in the middle of the hurt.

Thank you for listening to mine.

With all my heart,
Liliana Caliente-Cazadora

Part I: Shadows in the Living Room

I Was Nine and Already a Mother
Age 9

No one handed me the job.
No one said,
"Here, raise him."
But I did.

Because someone had to.

I packed Miguel's lunch
when Mom forgot.
Taught him how to brush his teeth,
tie his shoes,
wait for the microwave to beep
before opening it.

I read him bedtime stories
with one ear open
for slamming doors,
for glass hitting tile,
for the creak of danger
coming down the hall.

I lied for her.
To his teachers,
to the neighbor,
to him.

"She's just tired."
"She didn't mean it."
"She's okay."

I held him when he cried.
Wiped his face,
told him he was safe
even when I wasn't sure.

I folded his laundry,
fixed his socks to match,
made little games
out of silence
so he wouldn't notice
how loud the fear had gotten.

And when Mom locked herself
in her room for hours,
I made peanut butter sandwiches
and let Miguel pick
which half he wanted first
so he'd feel like
he had a choice.

I didn't know it then,
but I was building
a version of home
out of crumbs
and carefulness.

I was nine,
and already
a mother.

The Day They Took My Father
Age 14

It was still light out.
Too early for goodbyes,
too bright for handcuffs.

I watched from the hallway,
bare feet on cool tile,
while the officers filled the doorway
like they belonged more than he did.

He didn't yell.
Didn't resist.
Just looked at Mom
like she'd finally won something.
Like they were keeping score
and this was the last point.

Miguel was upstairs,
face buried in comics.
I told him not to come down,
and he didn't ask why.
That was the first time
he obeyed without question.

They didn't slam the door.
Didn't explain.
And I didn't cry
until I heard the car drive away—
because then it was real.
Not just a bad day.
Not just a warning.

Just gone.

Mom lit a cigarette
before the engine faded.
Sat on the armrest
like she needed something unstable
to keep her upright.
She didn't look at me.
Not once.

She just said,
"Well. That's done."
Like we'd dropped off dry cleaning.

That night,
the house felt emptier than ever,
even though one less person
should have made it easier to breathe.

But it wasn't relief.
It was the kind of silence
that knows
this is only the beginning
of what's about to break.

Miguel Slept Through the Sirens
Age 14

He was still in pajamas.
One sock on.
Cheeks flushed from sleep
and dreams I hoped were nothing like mine.

The sirens had come and gone,
red light dancing across the walls
like a warning I was too late to read.
But he didn't wake up.
He never did when it mattered.

I used to think that made him lucky.
Now I know
it just made him easy to protect.

I sat on the edge of his bed
for twelve minutes
after they took Dad.
Watched his chest rise and fall,
slow and steady,
like nothing had changed
and maybe that made it true.

I thought about what I'd say
when he asked where Dad went.
I didn't want to lie,
but I couldn't tell him
what I'd seen in his eyes
before the door closed.
The rage.
The shame.
The relief.

I whispered,
"I've got you,"
though he couldn't hear me.
Though I didn't know
how much I had left to give.

He rolled over,
murmured something about cartoons,
and I wished for a world
where he could stay that small
a little longer.

Where sirens meant help,
not history.

Where big sisters
didn't have to become mothers
overnight.

How to Listen Without Looking
Age 10–14

In our house,
you learned early
that sound
meant everything.

A drawer opened too fast?
Duck.
A beer can cracked before noon?
Disappear.
A certain tone in Mom's voice—
low and sweet—
meant she was already three drinks in,
and the sweetness wouldn't last.

You listened with your skin.
Your stomach.
That part of your chest
where fear first shows up
before it has a name.

I knew which footsteps
belonged to anger
and which to exhaustion.
I knew the way keys sounded
when they dropped on the counter—
whether someone was home
or just passing through.

I stopped watching TV
with the volume up.
I stopped singing in the shower.
I stopped letting the microwave beep.

Quiet wasn't calm.
It was preparation.

Silence
was where you braced.
Listened.
Waited.

There were nights
I lay still in bed
counting each floorboard creak
like a prayer.
Wishing it would skip our room.
Wishing I could pull the noise
out of the air
and swallow it
before it became something worse.

By the time I was twelve,
I could sense a fight
before a word was spoken.
By thirteen,
I knew when to disappear.
By fourteen,
I was already invisible.

And that's how I survived.
Not by running—
but by hearing
everything
before it broke.

Mom Was Louder After the Liquor
Age 11–14

She didn't need to scream.
Not at first.
Her voice just stretched wider,
like the liquor gave it room
to roam the walls.

She'd sing while cooking—
off-key, off-rhythm—
spatula in one hand,
bottle sweating on the counter.
We learned to laugh when she laughed.
That was safer.
That was code.

But by the third drink,
her laugh turned sharp,
and the room turned with her.
Jokes became traps.
Questions became crimes.
Miguel learned to nod,
even when he didn't understand.

She called me "smart girl"
when she was one glass in,
and "mouthy brat"
when the bottle got lighter.

Her footsteps got heavier.
Her hugs too tight.
Her silence—
the kind you could choke on.

Some nights,
she'd knock over chairs

just trying to walk straight.
Other nights,
she'd sit on the couch
and talk to no one
for hours.

I memorized her liquor levels
like clockwork.
Learned which slur
meant she'd start crying,
and which one
meant she wouldn't.

I used to think
it was my job
to keep her calm.
That if I said the right thing
or cleaned the counter
just in time,
she'd stay soft.

But softness never stayed.
Not in her.
Not in that house.
Not for long.

Part II: Things My Mother Left Behind

She Was Still Warm When I Found Her
Age 16

I thought she was sleeping.
That's the first lie I told myself.
Even with the door cracked,
I knew something was wrong.

The TV was still buzzing.
Static humming like it knew.
Her cigarette burned down to ash
on the tray beside her,
still holding its shape
like it hadn't realized
she was done.

She was on the couch.
Not sprawled—
just… slumped.
Like her body had folded in on itself,
tired of being a home for pain.

I said her name twice
before I crossed the room.
The third time,
my voice cracked.
The fourth,
I was already crying.

She was still warm
when I touched her.
Still smelled like the vanilla lotion
she always put on before bed.
Her chest
didn't rise.
Her eyes
didn't flutter.

But she was warm.
And for a moment,
I thought that meant hope.

I don't remember the phone call.
Just Miguel asking if Mom was okay.
And me saying,
"Don't come in here."
Over and over
until he stopped asking.

I sat with her
for seventeen minutes
before anyone came.
And for years
I would count to seventeen
when I needed to remember
how long it took
to lose everything.

They said it was accidental.
The mix of pills and vodka.
But nothing about her felt accidental.

She left us quietly.
Like she always did.
One door at a time.
One bottle at a time.
One apology she never made.

And I was sixteen
and shaking
and full of silence
and already half-grown
from everything I'd carried.

But that morning,
with the sun rising
like it didn't care,
I became something else entirely.

The girl who found her mother
still warm,
but already
gone.

No One Tells You What to Do With the Body
Age 16

She was still there.
Still in the living room.
Still wearing that oversized sweatshirt
with the coffee stain on the sleeve.
Still holding the shape
of someone who might wake up.

But she wasn't.
And I didn't know what to do.

They don't teach this in school—
how to sit with death
before it's officially pronounced.
How to keep breathing
when your mother's heart has stopped.

I thought about calling 911,
but I didn't know
what to say.
Would they come faster
if I cried?
Would they believe me
if I didn't?

I checked her pulse twice.
Held her hand.
Said her name
like maybe it was a spell
that could bring her back.

And then I waited.
Not for her.
But for the world
to do something about it.

The paramedics were quiet.
The questions were not.
"Was she sick?"
"Was she using?"
"Was she alone?"

I wanted to scream.
No.
She wasn't alone.
I was here.
I've always been here.

But no one asked about me.
Only about the body.

I stood in the hallway
while strangers took her away.
Watched the corners of the couch
where she'd sat the night before.
Still warm.
Still stained with the weight of her.

I thought grief would feel louder.

But that day,
it felt like nothing.
Like breathing in
and never exhaling.

The Cabinet Wasn't Locked Anymore
Age 16

After they took her,
I stood in front of the cabinet
where she kept the pills.

She used to keep it locked—
a tiny brass latch,
a squeaky hinge,
a warning built into the wood.

I used to think it was to protect us.

Now I know
it was to hide from herself.

I opened it
just to see.
The bottles were still there—
half full,
names I couldn't pronounce,
labels curling at the corners
like even they were tired.

One of them was open.
Cap loose,
a few pills spilled
like they'd tried to crawl away.

I didn't cry.
Not then.

Just stood there,
looking at the shelf
like it might explain something.
Like if I stared long enough,

the medicine would speak.
Tell me what she needed
so badly to escape.

There was a candy tin
tucked behind the bottles.
Empty.
Like everything else.

I closed the door
without locking it.
Because it didn't matter anymore.

She didn't need it locked
to keep us out.
She was already gone.

And I didn't need
another place
to store her secrets.

Final Dose, Final Silence
Age 16

The death certificate
came in the mail
like a bill.

A plain envelope
with her name printed in black
as if that's all she ever was.
Not "Mom."
Not even "Mother."
Just a legal name
no one used in real life.

I opened it alone.

There it was:
Cause of death:
Accidental overdose.
Time of death:
6:14 a.m.
Found by:
Daughter.

That last word
sat on the page
like an accusation.

It didn't say
she used to braid my hair
with shaky hands.
Didn't say
she liked lemon in her tea
or that her laugh could fill a room
on good days.

It didn't say
I held her hand
until it went cold.
That I whispered her name
long after it stopped meaning anything.

Just
Accidental.

Like she tripped
and fell
into forever.

I stared at that paper
for twenty minutes.
Like it might change
if I blinked hard enough.
If I rewrote her
with my breath.

But it didn't.
And I didn't.

Because the page
doesn't hold grief.
It only holds
what fits in the margins.

And my mother
was never small enough
to be measured
by lines.

Sergio Never Asked Me to Explain
Age 16

We packed two bags.
One for me.
One for Miguel.
That's all we had time for
before the social worker arrived.

I remember looking around the house—
the couch where she died,
the broken cabinet,
a bowl of cereal going soggy on the counter—
and realizing
none of it felt like home anymore.

Uncle Sergio met us at the front step
like he'd been waiting
long before the call.

He didn't say,
"I'm sorry."
He didn't say,
"What happened?"

He just opened the door,
moved a pile of jackets from the couch,
and said,
"This is yours now."

Miguel clung to him.
Like it was safe
to hold on to something.

I stood in the doorway longer.
Didn't know

how to walk into calm
without flinching.

That first night,
there was soup.
And silence.
But not the kind
that comes before yelling.
The kind that says,
"You can rest now."

Sergio didn't ask questions.
He didn't need to.
He let us be quiet
without making it uncomfortable.

He bought Miguel new shoes
before school started.
Asked what color he liked.
Let him pick.

No one had asked Miguel
what he liked in a long time.

And for the first time,
in years maybe,
I slept through the night
without checking the locks.

Part III: Unwritten Reports

The Night My Voice Froze
Age 19

He was someone I knew.
Not well,
but enough to laugh at his jokes in class,
enough to think
I was safe in his dorm room.

I said no.
I remember that.

Not loud.
Not firm.
But I said it.

He smiled
like I'd just told a story
he wasn't done interrupting.

And then—
my voice left me.

Like it stepped out of the room
so my body could take
what was coming
alone.

I left my body that night.
Watched it from the ceiling
like a stranger.
Watched my limbs go still
while my mind screamed
in a voice
no one else could hear.

I didn't bleed.
Not in the way
people think you should.
But I bled in silence
for months.

I showered
three times a day.
Scrubbed the places
he had touched
until my skin forgot
how to be soft.

And when I passed him
in the hallway two days later,
he said,
"Hey, you."
Like nothing happened.
Like I was still a person
he had the right to greet.

I wanted to say something.
Anything.

But my voice
was still frozen.

I Was the Only Witness and Still No One Believed Me
Age 19

I told a friend.
She said,
"Are you sure it was… that?"
Like I might have misunderstood
the way my body locked itself
to survive.

I told a professor.
He looked uncomfortable.
Changed the subject.
Said he'd connect me with someone.
He never did.

I filled out the form
in the campus clinic—
checked "yes" next to
Have you experienced sexual assault?
and "no" next to
Would you like to file a report?

I wanted to write:
What's the point?

I imagined the questions.
What were you wearing?
Did you say no loud enough?
Why didn't you scream?
Why didn't you run?
Are you sure
you didn't lead him on?

I've heard those questions
asked of other girls
by other men

wearing badges
or holding clipboards.

I already knew
how this story would end—
with him walking free
and me
walking around campus
like a ghost.

So I said nothing.

Because I was the only witness.
And even I
wasn't sure
I'd be believed.

His Wedding Ring Wasn't My Sin
Age 20

He never took it off.
The ring.
Silver.
Simple.
It caught the light
even when the room was dark.

He said he loved her.
Said it like a promise
he kept breaking
with every glance
he gave me.

I believed him.
Or maybe I just believed
that I could be enough
for someone,
even for a moment.

He called me
complicated.
Magnetic.
Dangerous.
But he never called me
at night.

We met in coffee shops
too far from campus.
In parking lots
where no one knew our names.
In text messages
that disappeared by morning.

I told myself
I didn't want more.
That I could hold the pieces
he offered
without bleeding.

But I did.

Because I wasn't the sin.
His choices weren't mine.
But the guilt clung to me
like smoke.

When it ended,
he said,
"You'll understand one day."

But I already did.
I understood loneliness
better than he ever would.

And I knew what it felt like
to be the thing someone wanted
when no one was watching.

She Kissed Me in a Library and I Thought, Maybe This Is Home
Age 20

It was between the poetry shelves.
A Tuesday.
Late afternoon,
sunlight slanting through the dusty glass.

She was reading Adrienne Rich.
I asked if she'd read Plath.
She smiled like I was quoting a secret
we both already knew.

She touched my arm
when she laughed.
Left her hand there
a second too long.
And that second
held everything
I hadn't let myself want.

When she kissed me,
it wasn't rushed.
Wasn't secret.
Wasn't shameful.
Just warm,
like her hands,
like her voice,
like the silence between us
that didn't need filling.

No one was watching.
And for once,
I didn't care if they were.

I didn't think about labels.
Or rules.
Or who I was supposed to be.
I just felt her lips
soft against mine
like a question
I didn't have to answer.

Afterward,
we sat on the floor
between stacks of books
and shared a coffee
like the world had slowed down
just for us.

It didn't last.
But for that moment,
it was real.

And for a girl
who'd spent her whole life
surviving love
that never stayed—

it felt like
home.

Unwritten Reports
Age 21

There are so many versions
of my story
that never made it to paper.

No official statements.
No case numbers.
No headlines.
Just moments
folded into silence
and placed carefully
on the shelf
next to things
I told myself didn't matter.

I never reported my father's fists.
Never documented
the bruises Mom left
with her words.
Never told the counselor
what the man in the dorm did.
I smiled.
I passed the test.
I kept my voice
where it couldn't be used against me.

There is no file for the nights
I woke up shaking.
No chart that lists
the taste of shame
after being someone's secret.
No form to track
how many times I've asked,
"Was it my fault?"

If I wrote them all down,
every time I stayed quiet,
the pages would fill
a room.

But they never asked.
And I never offered.
Because I learned early
that some stories
aren't taken seriously
unless you bleed in public
and cry on cue.

So I've kept them.
All of them.
Tucked beneath my ribs,
stacked behind my teeth,
written on the inside of my skin.

My body is the file.
My memory,
the witness.

And this—
this is the report
I was never allowed to write
until now.

Part IV:
The Women I Kissed, the Men I Survived

He Needed Me Until He Didn't
Age 22

He came to me
like a man falling
through his own life.
Divorce papers unsigned,
rent unpaid,
but his arms
always open.

He said I made things quiet.
Said I steadied him.
Said I was the only thing
that felt real.

And I believed him.
Because when you grow up
being the strong one,
you start mistaking
dependence
for love.

I made him dinner.
Held his hand
when the panic attacks hit.
Slept beside him
while he talked in his sleep
about another woman's name.

I kept thinking
that if I loved him better,
softer,
he'd stay.

But one day,
he just stopped calling.

No fight.
No tears.
Just silence.

I ran into him weeks later.
He said,
"I'm doing better now,"
like I should be proud.
Like that was what I was there for—
to patch him up
and send him on his way.

That night,
I stared at the ceiling
and wondered
why I always end up
being the place
men rest
before they return
to the lives they left behind.

She Didn't Call Me Her Girlfriend But I Knew
Age 22

We never made it official.
Never changed our status,
never took selfies,
never posted anything
that couldn't be explained away
as friendship.

But I knew.

I knew in the way
she touched the back of my neck
when no one was looking.
I knew in the way
she whispered my name
like it was a dare
she wasn't brave enough to say aloud.

We shared beds,
meals,
books with underlined lines
that said things
we couldn't.

She told me
I made her feel safe.
Told me
I was a secret worth keeping.
Like that was a compliment.

We went to the movies
but sat apart.
Went to parties
but arrived in different cars.

She called me "her person"
but never "her love."

And I let it happen.
Because part of me
was still used to being
half-held.
Half-claimed.
Half-loved.

When she stopped texting,
she didn't explain.
And I didn't ask.
Because what would I say?

We weren't together.
Not really.
But when she left,
it still felt
like a breakup.

I Am Not the Secret Anymore
Age 23

I used to let them love me
in whispers—
back seats,
late-night texts,
weekends when their real lives
were busy
being something else.

I convinced myself
that stolen hours
still counted as love.
That if they held me
like they meant it,
even behind closed doors,
it was enough.

But I got tired
of being the parentheses
in someone else's sentence.
The asterisk
at the bottom of their truth.

I started saying no.
Started asking,
"Will you take my hand
when the lights are on?"
"Will you say my name
without flinching?"

Some of them didn't answer.
Some walked away.
Some told me
I was asking for too much.

But I wasn't.

I was asking to exist.
Out loud.
Fully.
Without apology.

So I stopped being the secret.
Stopped folding myself
into corners.
Stopped dimming my light
so someone else could sleep easy.

I am not shame.
I am not regret.
I am not the thing
you only want
when no one is watching.

I am here.
In the open.
And I will not go quiet
for anyone.

The Shape of Need
Age 23

I used to think love
looked like the people
who showed up
after midnight.

Like attention
meant affection.
Like being wanted
meant being safe.

But that wasn't love.
It was need.
And it had a shape.
Sharp.
Narrow.
Always just out of reach.

Need looked like
his hand on my hip
when he couldn't sleep.
Like her smile
in a room full of strangers
that vanished
the moment we stepped outside.

Need sounded like
"Don't tell anyone."
Like "Let's keep this just between us."
Like "You're the only one who gets me,"
spoken between excuses
and absences.

It felt like hunger.
Gnawing.

Insatiable.
The kind that doesn't go away
just because someone touches you.

And I fed it.
With silence.
With surrender.
With every part of myself
I thought I could spare
to be loved.

But need
is not the same as love.
It's a shadow of it.
A trick of the light.

And I am learning
to want something gentler.
To wait for something
that doesn't
leave me empty.

Loving Doesn't Mean Staying
Age 24

He wasn't cruel.
Not loud.
Not sharp.
Not the kind of man
you warn your friends about.

He was kind
in the way that makes you hesitate
to name what's missing.
He remembered birthdays.
Held doors.
Made tea
when I couldn't sleep.

But still—
I was disappearing.

Slowly.
Quietly.
Like mist on a mirror.

He wanted comfort.
I wanted connection.
He wanted someone easy.
I wanted someone real.

And I kept trying
to shrink myself
into a version
that didn't ask too much.

Until one night,
I looked at myself in the mirror
and didn't recognize the woman

folding her needs
into smaller and smaller corners.

I loved him.
That was the truth.

But I was beginning to love myself, too.
And the version of me
he could live with
was not the version
I could live as.

So I left.
Not because I stopped loving him,
but because I finally started
loving me.

And now I know—
loving someone
doesn't mean
you have to stay.

Especially
when staying
means leaving yourself behind.

Part V: Soft Power

He Let Me Sleep Without Worrying About Locks
Age 16–17

His house smelled like coffee
and old books.
Soft lighting.
Quiet hallways.
Nothing slammed.

The first night,
I didn't sleep.
I lay in bed listening
for footsteps,
for anger,
for the creak of something coming.

But nothing came.

Just the hum of a fan,
the sound of Miguel breathing
in the room next door,
and the faint knock
of Sergio checking in
without opening the door.

He didn't ask for stories.
Didn't pry open wounds.
He just made space
for us to rest.

There were no locks on our bedroom doors.
But somehow,
I felt safer
than I ever had
with all the deadbolts in the world.

He never raised his voice.
Never cursed at the walls
or flung silence like a weapon.

He just made pancakes on Sundays,
bought us notebooks for school,
and made sure Miguel had shoes
that fit.

That winter,
for the first time in my life,
I slept
without my hands clenched.
Without one ear open.
Without a plan to run.

And that was love,
though no one ever said it aloud.
Just the kind
that doesn't ask for anything
but your breath.

Diego Calls Me Tía and I Cry
Age 25

He says it like it's always been true.
Like I've always been
the one who shows up
with juice boxes and crayons,
with stories that don't end in silence.

"Tía,"
he calls,
arms wide,
sticky fingers outstretched
like love is easy,
like love is safe.

And I cry.

Not the loud kind.
Not the shaking kind.
But the kind that leaks
from a place so deep
you didn't know
it was still wounded.

Because he doesn't know
what I saved Miguel from.
Doesn't know
the doors I held shut
so my brother could sleep.
Doesn't know
how many nights I prayed
for a future
that didn't look like the past.

And here it is—
this wide-eyed boy

with his father's laugh
and his mother's grace.

Running barefoot in a yard
that feels nothing like our old one.
Pointing at the sky
like the clouds belong to him.

He doesn't flinch
at sudden sounds.
Doesn't check faces
before he speaks.
Doesn't carry
what we carried.

And that,
right there,
is the miracle.

Not that I survived—
but that he
never had to.

The First Time I Slept Without Fear
Age 24

It wasn't loud.
Wasn't a revelation.
Just a night
like any other.
Except it wasn't.

I brushed my teeth,
turned off the light,
and didn't check the locks
twice.
Didn't peek out the window
to see if something waited.
Didn't brace myself
for the past
to crawl back in.

I pulled the blanket up,
tucked it beneath my chin
like I used to when I was little
and still believed
blankets could protect me.

And then—
I closed my eyes.
And nothing screamed inside me.

No memories chasing the dark.
No heartbeat
thudding like footsteps
down the hall.

Just breath.
Mine.
Steady.

Soft.
Uninterrupted.

And I thought—
maybe this is healing.

Not fireworks.
Not forgiveness.
Just the quiet
that comes
when survival
is no longer
the only thing
you know how to do.

I Don't Apologize for My Joy Anymore
Age 25

There was a time
I laughed
and then looked around
to see if it was allowed.

A time when joy
felt like betrayal—
to the girl I used to be,
to the people who never got this far.

But not anymore.

Now I dance in my kitchen
with my socks sliding across tile.
Now I wear red lipstick
just because it makes me feel
like I survived something
and came out glowing.

I eat dessert first.
Say no without flinching.
Say yes
without checking if it makes anyone uncomfortable.

I let people take photos of me
and don't ask to see them first.
I let the light in.
I let the mirror be kind.
I let myself want
and dream
and rest.

Because I've carried enough.

Carried guilt,
carried silence,
carried other people's comfort
on my back
like a burden I didn't ask for.

But now—
I carry joy.
And it fits me.

It doesn't need to be quiet.
It doesn't need permission.
It just needs space.

And I've made room.

This Time, I Choose Me
Age 26

I used to shape myself
to fit what others needed.
Soft here,
small there.
Bending like light
through a cracked window.

I said yes
when I wanted to scream.
Stayed
when I should have run.
Loved
when I was empty.

I gave pieces away
like they grew back overnight.
They didn't.

But now—
now I know better.

This time,
I listen to my own voice
before anyone else's.
This time,
I leave when it starts to hurt
instead of waiting
to be broken.

I speak the truth,
even when it shakes.
I want what I want,
without explaining why.
I rest

without earning it.
I forgive myself
without conditions.

This time,
I don't beg to be chosen.

I am the choice.

I am the home
I've been searching for.
I am the love
I tried to earn
from the ones who never knew
how to hold me.

This time,
I choose me.

And I'm staying.

Author's Note

If you've made it to this page,
thank you — truly.

This book was not easy to write.
These poems came from places I tried to bury for years —
memories I kept in shadow,
fears I convinced myself were weakness,
and truths I once thought would make me unlovable.

But silence doesn't heal you.
It just keeps the pain from breathing.
So I wrote.

I wrote for the girl I used to be,
who held in too much
and apologized for taking up space.
I wrote for the women
who have carried the weight of unspoken things,
and for the men and nonbinary souls
who have survived without softness.

I wrote for my brother Miguel,
who gave me a reason to keep going.
And for the woman I've become —
not perfect,
not finished,
but finally whole enough
to love herself out loud.

If something in these pages made you feel seen,
held,
or even just a little less alone,
then the story was worth telling.

This is not the end.
Just the beginning
of speaking
without fear.

With love and truth,
Liliana Caliente-Cazadora

Q&A with the Author

Liliana Caliente-Cazadora answers questions about her poetic memoir

Q: Why did you choose poetry to tell your story instead of prose?
A: Poetry gave me the freedom to speak without needing to explain. Sometimes trauma doesn't fit neatly into paragraphs or chapters — it comes in fragments, flashes, and breathless moments. Poetry let me tell the truth in pieces, and sometimes that's the only way it can be told.

Q: Was there a poem that was the hardest to write?
A: Yes — *"She Was Still Warm When I Found Her."* Writing that poem meant reliving the exact moment I lost my mother. I had avoided it for years, but once I wrote it, something inside me shifted. It didn't erase the pain, but it let me carry it differently.

Q: How long did it take to write this collection?
A: I've been carrying these poems inside me for most of my life. But once I committed to writing the book, it came together over several months. Some poems poured out in minutes. Others took weeks. I let the process guide me, not the clock.

Q: What does the title mean to you?
A: *I Am the Story I Was Afraid to Tell* is more than a title — it's a truth I didn't know I was ready to claim. For so long, I believed my past defined me in the worst way. But writing this book helped me realize that I'm not just what happened to me — I'm who I became in spite of it.

Q: What do you hope readers take away from this book?
A: I hope they feel less alone. I hope they find pieces of themselves in these poems and realize that their pain, their silence, their survival — it all matters. And I hope it gives someone permission to tell their own story, in whatever form it needs to take.

Q: Will there be more books?
A: Yes. I don't know what form it'll take yet, but I know I'm not done writing. There's more to explore — especially love, fear, heartache, recovery and joy without apology. I've spent so much time surviving. Now, I want to write about living.

About the Author

Liliana Caliente-Cazadora is a poet, storyteller, and survivor whose words are rooted in lived experience. She grew up in the shadows of addiction, grief, and silence—but found her voice through poetry and the power of truth.

A graduate with a degree in English, Liliana writes from the intersections of trauma, identity, queerness, and resilience. Her work explores the spaces between what is spoken and what is buried, drawing from her own journey through loss, heartbreak, survival, and healing.

When she isn't writing, she's sipping strong coffee, journaling under a quiet sky, or spending time with her chosen family—including her younger brother Miguel, who inspires many of her most tender lines.

Resources & Support

If you are struggling with trauma, abuse, grief, or emotional distress, you are not alone.
Below are resources that offer support, connection, and help — no matter where you are on your journey.

Crisis & Emotional Support

National Suicide & Crisis Lifeline (U.S.)
Call or text 988 — Available 24/7
988lifeline.org

RAINN (Rape, Abuse & Incest National Network)
National Sexual Assault Hotline: 1-800-656-HOPE (4673)
Live chat and resources at rainn.org

Crisis Text Line
Text HOME to 741741 — 24/7 support via text
crisistextline.org

For Survivors of Abuse, Trauma, or Neglect

The National Domestic Violence Hotline
Call 1-800-799-SAFE (7233) or text START to 88788
thehotline.org

1in6
Support for male survivors of sexual trauma
1in6.org

Pandora's Project
Online support for survivors of sexual assault
pandys.org

LGBTQ+ Support

The Trevor Project (LGBTQ+ Youth)
Call 1-866-488-7386 or text START to 678678
thetrevorproject.org

Trans Lifeline
Peer support from trans volunteers
U.S.: 877-565-8860 | Canada: 877-330-6366
translifeline.org

Please remember:

Asking for help is not weakness.
You are not a burden.
And you never have to carry your pain alone.

For After the Last Page

for anyone still finding their way

May you forgive yourself
for the ways you survived.

May you lay down what was never yours to carry.

May you speak your truth
without fear of echo or silence.

May you find rest
in the spaces that once held your pain.

May you learn to trust your own voice
and the wisdom in your scars.

May you feel worthy
even when you're still healing.

May you remember—
you do not have to be whole
to be holy to yourself.

You are already enough.
You are already free.